Arnie Lightning

CHOMPY THE SHARK

Table of Contents

Chompy the Lonely Shark

Chompy the shark frowned to himself as he swam through the tropical ocean. All around him, he saw groups of friends—dolphins and seahorses and fish of all different sizes and colors. They were laughing and playing and having a grand old time. But whenever they saw Chompy, they began to panic and swim for cover.

Their actions made Chompy feel like crying. He understood why they were afraid; after all, sharks didn't have a very good reputation in the ocean. But

Chompy wished they would at least give him a chance. Long ago, he had decided not to be like the other sharks in his family. He had decided to be a vegetarian shark, who ate only underwater plants and never bothered the other sea creatures at all.

Chompy's family had been upset about his decision—so upset, in fact, that they began to make fun of Chompy. Chompy was so hurt by their nasty words that he left his family and set out on his own. At first, he'd thought that he would find some other sharks who didn't want to hurt other sea creatures, either. But none of the sharks he met were like that. When they learned that Chompy ate only plants, they made just as much fun of him as his family had.

Between all of the other sharks in the ocean, who laughed at Chompy, and the rest of the sea creatures, who were afraid and ran away from Chompy, Chompy began to believe that he'd never make friends. A tear slid down Chompy's face and mixed with the saltwater all around him.

Just then, Chompy spotted someone swimming his way. Unlike most of the other creatures Chompy saw, this swordfish was all alone. He was frowning, and he looked as unhappy as Chompy felt.

"Just wait till he sees me," Chompy thought. "He'll swim for his life!"

But, to Chompy's surprise, the swordfish's face lit up at the sight of him. He started swimming faster in Chompy's direction. "Hey!" he called. "Can I talk to you for a minute?"

Chompy was so happy and surprised that someone wanted to talk to him. "Sure!" he cried.

"Boy, oh, boy!" the swordfish gasped excitedly. "I can't believe it! A real-life shark who will actually give me the time of day! All the other sharks I try to talk to either ignore me or try to eat me! I've always dreamed of this day—talking to the king of the sea, the feared beast of the deep, the—"

"Excuse me?" Chompy asked, cutting him off.

The swordfish blushed. "Oh. I should probably introduce myself. I'm Buzz, and…well, I've always wished I could be a shark—so big and powerful! I know that's not possible, so the second-best thing would be to make friends with a shark. Will you be my friend?"

"I'd love to!" Chompy beamed. He introduced himself and went on to tell Buzz about his vegetarian lifestyle and how the other sharks made fun of him, and everyone else was afraid of him. "I've been lonely and friendless for so long," he finished sadly.

Buzz grinned. "Not anymore!" he exclaimed. "Let me introduce you to my best buds—Jilly the jellyfish, Slick the seal, and Flashy the starfish. We're a tough crowd—sharks don't scare us, especially vegetarian ones! Once you're a part of my group, you'll never be lonely again!"

This sounded like a dream-come-true to Chompy. "I hope you're right," he said excitedly.

And do you know what? He was!

Jilly the Dancing Jellyfish

"Very good, dancers!" Madame Jellee cried. A dozen little jellyfish swished around her, waving their tentacles gracefully. "Now, I would like to announce the cast of the Jellee Underwater Dance Academy's upcoming production of Jelly Lake."

Jilly the jellyfish felt her heart pound faster. This was the moment they had all been waiting for. A week ago, Jilly and the others had auditioned for roles in the big dance show. Today, they would find out who had the starring role.

Jilly waited patiently as Madame Jellee assigned roles to several of her classmates. Finally, she reached the end of her list. "And lastly," she declared, "the role of Jelette will be danced by Jilly."

Jilly couldn't believe it; she was the star of the show! As soon as class had ended, Jilly swam home quickly to share her news with her best friends Buzz the swordfish, Flashy the starfish, Slick the seal, and Chompy the shark.

They were all thrilled for her. "We'll be right there in the front row to cheer you on!" declared Chompy.

Jilly beamed. Chompy was the newest member of her friend group, and he fit in perfectly. "Thanks, you guys!"

Every day for the next two weeks, Jilly practiced her dancing. She practiced at the Dance Academy, and at home. She practiced in front of her classmates and her friends, and she practiced all by herself.

On the day of the show, Madame Jellee swished backstage to encourage Jilly. "You are a beautiful dancer, Jilly," she said. "You have practiced so hard. Go out there this afternoon and dance with confidence. There's nothing to be afraid of."

There's nothing to be afraid of. Madame's words echoed in Jilly's head. She hadn't felt the least bit nervous all this time—but suddenly, she was terrified! She couldn't go out there and dance in front of that huge audience! What if she messed up? What if—?

"I'm sorry!" Jilly blurted to Madame. "I can't be Jelette!"

Madame gasped. "Why not?"

Jilly didn't stay to answer. She swam into the audience and found her friends. "We're going home now," Jilly whimpered. "I'm too scared to be Jelette."

Jilly expected her friends to support her decision—but, to her surprise, they were upset!

"I'm not leaving this theater until you dance up there on that stage!" declared Buzz.

"And the same goes for us!" chimed the others.

"You'll be sorry if you don't do this," Chompy added quietly. "Sometimes the things we want most are also the scariest—like my decision to be a vegetarian shark."

Jilly thought about that. Chompy hadn't had any friends because of his decision—until he had met her group, that is. Now the whole underwater community loved Chompy. If Chompy could go after what he wanted in such a big way, there was no reason in the world that Jilly couldn't do the same.

She grinned at her friends, took a deep breath, and darted back to Madame Jellee.

"I changed my mind," she said, her heart still pounding.

Madame Jellee smiled and gave her a hug.

And to this day, no jellyfish at the Dance Academy has ever danced Jelette as beautifully as Jilly did that afternoon!

Just for Fun Activity

Jilly's friends encouraged her to do something she was afraid of doing. Have your friends and family ever encouraged you in a similar situation? Write a story or draw a picture about your own experience!

Buzz the Shark-Crazy Swordfish

Buzz the swordfish frowned as he peered at his reflection in a seashell-framed mirror. He was so obviously a swordfish; there was no way he would ever pass for a shark.

Buzz sighed. Ever since he was born, he had longed to be a shark. Sharks were so big and powerful. Buzz admired the way they commanded the attention of the entire ocean. Whenever someone saw a shark, they were sure to flee in terror. Whenever they saw a swordfish...well, most of them just didn't care one way or the other.

Buzz knew that wasn't true of his best friends Jilly the jellyfish, Flashy the starfish, Slick the seal, and Chompy the shark. They loved and supported Buzz no matter what.

Buzz smiled a little as he thought of Chompy. Chompy was his newest friend, and Buzz had been the first of the group to meet him. He had been so excited to make friends with a real, live shark. Chompy was the only shark Buzz had ever met who didn't ignore him or, even worse, try to eat him.

At first, it had been enough just to be friends with a shark—even though Chompy was hardly terrifying. But now, Buzz wanted more. He wanted to be a shark. Maybe Chompy could give him some pointers.

Buzz swam over to Chompy's place later that morning.

"Hi, Buzz!" called Chompy. "What's up?"

"Well, "Buzz began, "I was wondering if you could give me some advice?"

"I'd be glad to," Chompy smiled. "What sort of advice do you need?"

Buzz blushed. "Um…" he stammered, suddenly embarrassed, "well, uh, do you think you could tell me how to look and act more like a shark?"

Chompy's eyes bugged out. "I know you like sharks, Buzz. But why…?"

"I want to be mighty and powerful!" Buzz cut in. "I want to intimidate other sea creatures. It must be so dramatic and exciting."

Chompy sighed. "Many sea creatures are afraid of swordfish," he replied. "Isn't that enough? I don't like having others be afraid of me."

Buzz groaned. "You don't get it, Chompy. Sharks are so special and unique. They are so cool!"

"Well, I think swordfish are pretty cool, too," Chompy argued. "Did you know that they're one of the ten fastest sea creatures in the world? Why would you want to give up that kind of speed? Why would you want to give up being you?"

Buzz thought about that for a moment. He imagined looking into his seashell mirror and seeing a shark's face staring back at him. As cool as that might sound to him now…it wouldn't be right. Because Buzz wasn't meant to be a shark. He was meant to be a swordfish. And he sure loved swimming fast!

Slowly, Buzz started to smile. "You're right, Chompy!" he cried. "I guess I'm happy being a swordfish, after all."

"I'm glad," beamed Chompy. "Now that that's settled, I do have an idea for you. You know how Flashy is throwing a costume party next week?"

"Yeah," Buzz said slowly.

Chompy swam closer and whispered something to Buzz.

Buzz grinned so hard, it hurt his face.

And who do you suppose came to Flashy's costume party dressed up like a shark?

Just for Fun Activity

Use a paper plate, markers, glue, paper, and a little imagination to make an animal mask of your own. Have an adult help you cut eye-holes with scissors and attach ribbon or elastic to hold the mask to your head. You'll be all set for Flashy's costume party, yourself!

Slick the World-Traveling Seal

Slick the seal happily turned a somersault beneath the surface of the warm, tropical ocean. He smiled to himself as the warm sun hit his face. The sun was so strong here; it reached all the way down to the ocean floor. Slick couldn't imagine living anywhere else besides the tropics.

Smiling, Slick swam to his home, which was on the warm rocks along a beautiful white-sand beach. His family was already there, basking in the sunshine with their eyes closed. Slick sighed contentedly.

Later in the day, he would dive down deep and visit his undersea friends Chompy the shark, Buzz the swordfish, Jilly the jellyfish, and Flashy the starfish. But, for now, a nap in the tropical heat sounded wonderful.

Just as Slick was getting settled on his favorite rock, his little sister Slippery hurried over to him excitedly. "Slick!" she cried. "Mama and Papa got a message today from our cousins in the Arctic! They want us to visit them this summer!"

Slick gasped. "Are we going?"

Slippery nodded enthusiastically. "It's going to be our family vacation this year. We've never been to the Arctic before! And we haven't seen our cousins since they visited here when I was just a seal pup!" She clapped her flippers together. "Isn't it going to be great?"

Slick wasn't so sure about that. He knew that the Arctic was cold and icy. Why would anyone want to leave the beautiful tropics to visit such a frigid part of the world? He tried to smile, but inside, he was not excited at all.

That afternoon, Slick told his friends about his upcoming trip. "I'm not really looking forward to it," he admitted.

"But why not?" gasped Jilly. "The Arctic sounds exciting and exotic!"

"I wish I could visit!" added Buzz.

"Me, too!" said Chompy.

"It'll be so cool to see a completely different part of the world," Flashy put in with a dramatic sigh. "Be sure to send us sea-snail mail while you're gone!"

Slick groaned. His friends didn't get it at all.

Less than a week later, the seal family set off toward the Arctic. It was a long journey, but they stopped along the way to rest in different places. They stayed at beaches in Mexico and the United States and Canada. They made friends with seals and other creatures everywhere they went. They swam in different waters and enjoyed different types of seafood. As they continued along, the water grew colder and colder.

At last, they had arrived in the Arctic. Their family there was so happy to see them!

"Is that you, Slick?" his cousin Seymour cried.

Slick's eyes lit up. Seymour was just his age, and they hadn't seen each other in forever! It wasn't long before Slick, Slippery, and Seymour were playing together on the ice slides that the Arctic seals enjoyed, flip-flopping from iceberg to iceberg, and gobbling down specialty Arctic seafood.

Before he went to sleep that night, Slick smiled to himself, thinking of all the different adventures he had had so far. The trip from the tropics had been interesting and fun, and now that he and his family were here in the Arctic, it was so much better than Slick had ever expected!

His friends had been right: it really was special to see different parts of the world. He would write them some sea-snail mail tomorrow and tell them!

Flashy the TV-Starfish

"Tra-la-la!" Flashy the starfish sang loudly to herself. She was balanced on top of an underwater rock, which she was pretending was her stage. "Thank you, thank you very much," Flashy called to her imaginary audience. "Ladies and gentlefish, it is my pleasure to present to you this afternoon my very own, extraordinary, one-starfish production of Romeo and Starlet!"

With that, Flashy began to act out the play all by herself. She played the roles of both Romeo and Starlet, as well as all of the other characters. At the end of the tragic love story, Flashy threw herself dramatically back onto the rock.

Then she bobbed up, took a bow, and waved all five of her starfish rays at the audience that existed only in her imagination.

"Thank you, dah-lings!" Flashy called in a dramatic voice. She threw kisses to the fake crowd. "Muah, muah!"

Finally, Flashy gave herself a moment to relax. Acting was hard work. Ever since Flashy could remember, she had wanted to become a famous actress. But so far, the only real audience she ever got consisted of her best friends Chompy the shark, Jilly the jellyfish, Buzz the swordfish, and Slick the seal.

Even they hadn't been able to make it to this afternoon's performance of Romeo and Stariet…so why did Flashy suddenly hear applause? Real applause, not imaginary!

Before Flashy could wonder any longer, a professional-looking sea crab and her crew of assistants came into view from around a clump of underwater plants.

"That was spectacular!" the crab called out, continuing to clap. "You are a very talented young starfish," she told Flashy.

For once in her life, Flashy was speechless. She recognized that crab—Crabella Softshell, the famous director of Flashy's favorite TV show, Crabmore Girls! All Flashy could do was gasp. What was Crabella Softshell doing here?

As if she had read Flashy's mind, Crabella smiled and said, "Crabmore Girls is doing a special coral-reef shoot not far from here. It's a beautiful part of the ocean. My crew and I were just taking a lunch break when we heard you putting on your play." Crabella motioned at the producers, camerafish, and makeup artists who were with her.

"Wow," Flashy managed, finally finding her voice. "I…I can't believe it. I love Crabmore Girls!"

Crabella smiled. "Then you're just the young actress we've been looking for!"

Flashy gasped again. "What do you mean?"

"We need some extra actors for small parts in the coral-reef scene," Crabella explained. "Would you be interested?"

"Would I!" squealed Flashy.

The very next day, Flashy officially began her career as a professional actress. Even if she was just a kid playing a small part in one episode of a TV show, it was a special opportunity that she wouldn't have imagined in a million years!

As Flashy acted out the coral-reef scene with the stars of Crabmore Girls, her very best friends watched and silently cheered her on. Crabella had given them permission to visit the set, as long as they were quiet.

But as soon as Crabella yelled, "Cut!" Flashy's friends broke into cheers and applause.

Flashy grinned and took a bow. It was so nice to have a real, live audience for once!

Just for Fun Activity

In the story, Flashy acts out a play all by herself. Try acting out this story all by yourself, playing the roles of Flashy, Crabella, and Flashy's friends. It might be a lot to handle—but you can do it!

Funny Jokes for Kids

Q: Who do fish borrow money from?

A: The loan shark!

Q: What did the fish say when he got out of jail?

A: I'm off the hook!

Q: What is a knight's favorite fish?

A: A swordfish!

Q: What fish only swims at night?

A: A starfish!

Q: Why are fish so smart?

A: They are always in schools!

Q: What fish is best to have in a boat?

A: Sailfish!

Q: Why are fish so gullible?

A: They fall for things like hook, line, and sinker!

Q: How do you communicate with a fish?

A: You drop it a line!

Can you find your way through the maze?

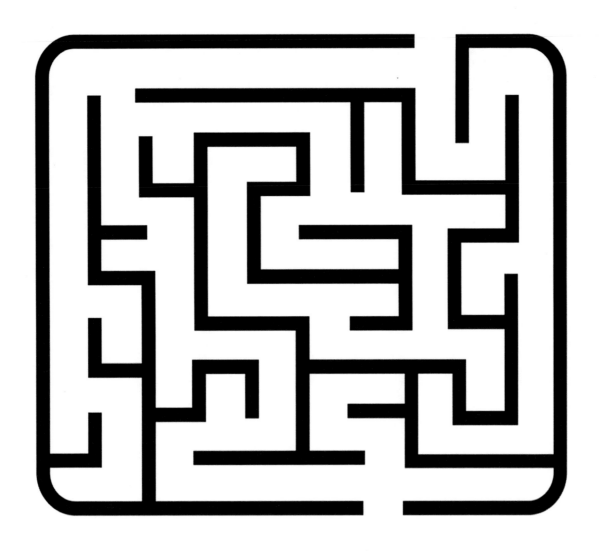

Can you find your way through the maze?

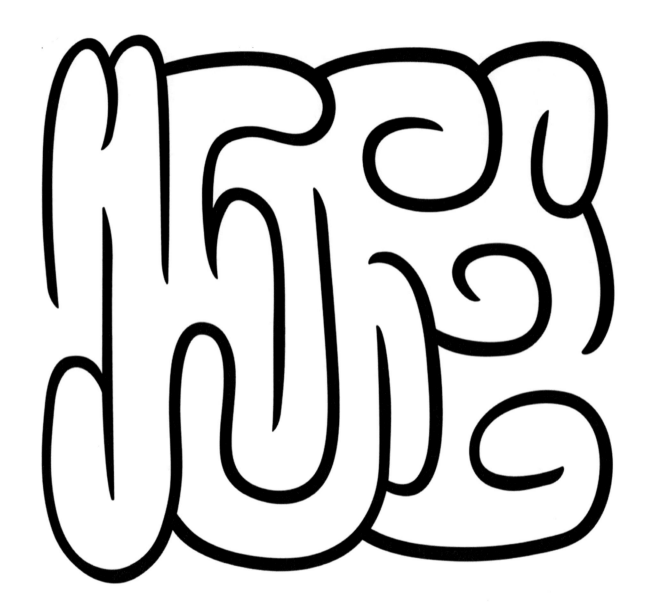

Can you find your way through the maze?

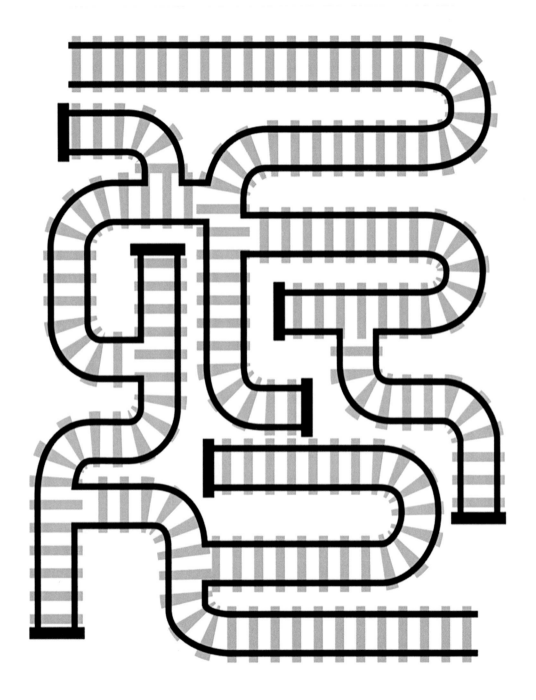

Can you find your way through the maze?

Maze Solutions

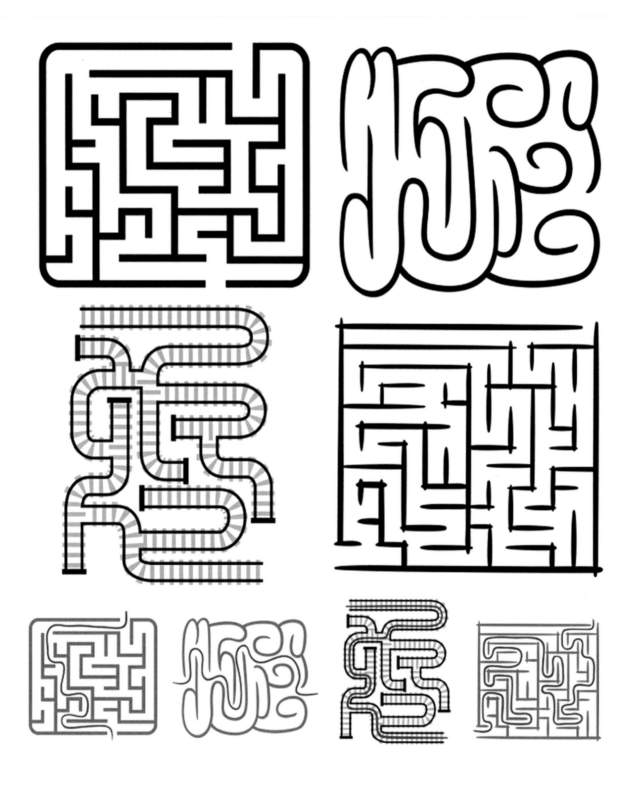

About the Author

Arnie Lightning is a dreamer. He believes that everyone should dream big and not be afraid to take chances to make their dreams come true.

Arnie enjoys writing, reading, doodling, and traveling. In his free time, he likes to play video games and run. Arnie lives in Mississippi where he graduated from The University of Southern Mississippi in Hattiesburg, MS.

For more information on the author, please visit:

www.ArnieLightning.com

Made in the USA
San Bernardino, CA
04 May 2019